To Mary, who listened all the way through.
A.F & P.P.

For Jane
K.L.

WAYLAND
338 Euston Road, London NW1 3BH
Wayland Australia, Level 17/207, Kent Street, Sydney, NSW 2000

First published in 2014 by Wayland

Text © Andrew Fusek Peters and Polly Peters 2014
Illustrations © Karin Littlewood 2014

Editor: Joyce Bentley
Designer: Paula Burgess

Dewey classification: 823.9'2-dc23

A CIP catalogue record of this book is available from the British Library.

ISBN 978 0 7502 8053 2
EBook ISBN 978 0 7502 8054 9
10 9 8

Printed and bound in Great Britain by Bell & Bain Ltd, Glasgow

Wayland is a division of Hachette Children's Books,
an Hachette UK company.
www.hachette.co.uk

The COLOUR THIEF

A family's story of depression

Andrew Fusek Peters
& Polly Peters

illustrated by
Karin Littlewood

WAYLAND
www.waylandbooks.co.uk

My dad's life was full of colour.
Every day, clouds smiled at him and trees waved hello.
We went walking together. We saw green hills
snoozing in the afternoon light, and
bright flowers singing to the sun.

But one day, Dad was full up
with sadness, all the way to the top.
He said his sky had turned grey.

I thought I had done something wrong,
but he told me I hadn't.

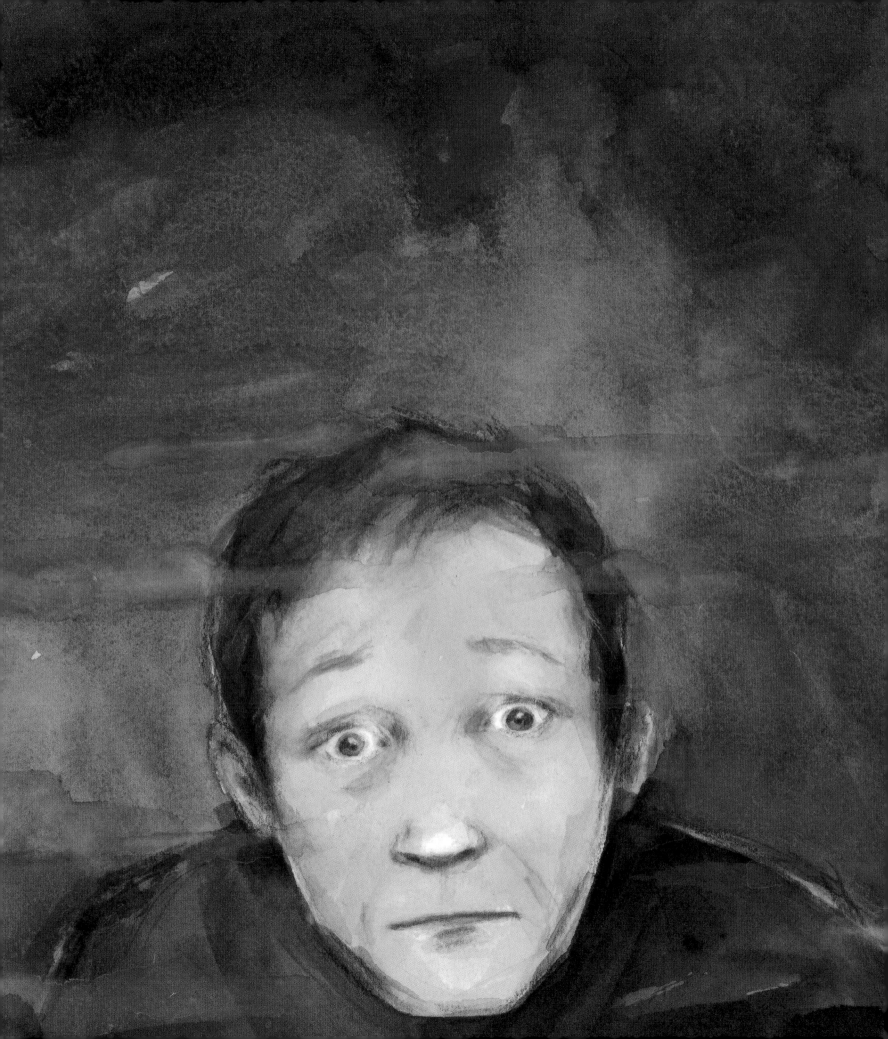

Soon, every day was a sad day for Dad.
He only saw the sun sulking, clouds
frowning, rain crying. We didn't go walking.
We didn't do anything together any more.

Outside, the trees stood silently, shaking their heads.
Dad stayed indoors and looked out of the window.

He said that if he went out, the lamp posts
would laugh at him or the streets would call him names.

I thought I had done something wrong, but he told me I hadn't.

He said that all the colours had gone.
Someone had stolen them away; just taken them
one by one. He said he felt sad and stuck,
like a marble in a bottle.

When the phone rang,
he told it to go away.

When the doorbell buzzed,
he pretended not to hear it.

I gave him cuddles.
We all gave him cuddles.
But he put those hugs
away in a box.

Then he closed the curtains
and lay in bed all day.

I thought I had done something wrong, but he told me I hadn't.

I felt lonely. There was a heavy
stone feeling inside me and I missed my dad.
I missed the sound of his laugh and his smiling eyes.

I drew a picture of him inside a big ice cube.

Dad went to see important people at
a hospital. They told him he was very
poorly and gave him medicine for his mind.
And they found him someone to talk to,
someone who listened.

Days turned over slowly,
one page at a time.
Weeks rumbled past our front door.
Months were stretchy,
like chewing gum.

And then one day, Dad opened the
window and the sun crept into our house.
I made a cup of tea for him, with sugar,
and he said it tasted good.

The grey shadows in the corners of
the room grew smaller . . . and smaller.

I asked Dad if he
wanted to go for a little walk.
He said yes and I held his hand.

The sky winked a blue eye.
Clouds smiled and every
tree waved hello.

Dad looked around. Then he looked down at me
and picked me up in a great, big, squeezy hug.

My dad was back.

He even smiled a shaky smile.
And the colours were bright all around us.